LONGMAN

Robin Hood

Simplified by D K Swan
Illustrated by Chris Ryley

Longman

Longman Group UK Limited,
Longman House, Burnt Mill, Harlow,
Essex CM20 2JE, England
and Associated Companies throughout the world.

First published 1989

ISBN 0-582-52287-0

Set in 12/14 point Lintron 202 Versailles
Produced by Longman Group (FE) Limited
Printed in Hong Kong

Acknowledgements

The cover background is a wallpaper design called NUAGE,
courtesy of Osborne and Little plc.

Stage 1: 500 word vocabulary

Please look under *New words* at the back of this book
for explanations of words outside this stage.

Contents

Introduction

The Robin Hood stories come from the time we call the Middle Ages, about the years 1000 to 1500. They are "folk" stories. That is, they were told by – or to – the people of the small farms and villages. Not the rich. Not the lords and ladies. Not the people who could read and write, like the churchmen.

Most of the common people were poor. The men with power and riches were the lords and the owners of land. Some – but not all – churchmen had power and riches too. Only a few of the people with power did anything to help the poor.

When life is like that, the common people love to hear stories about a "folk hero" like Robin Hood. Very many countries have stories about folk heroes. Sometimes they are real people. Sometimes, as with Robin Hood, we don't know: was he a real person? The folk hero always wins in the fight against power that is unfairly used.

Folk heroes like Robin Hood help the common people when those with power are unjust. Those who hear the stories feel that the hero is "on our side".

The Robin Hood stories were first told as ballads. A ballad is a poem that tells a story, and at first it was sung. The second story in this book (*Robin Hood and Sir Richard of the Lee*) is taken from a ballad which began:

> Lithe[1] and listen, gentlemen
> That be of free-born blood.
> I'll tell you of a good yeoman,
> His name was Robin Hood.
>
> Robin was a proud outlaw
> The while he walked on ground.[2]
> So courteous[3] an outlaw as he was one
> Was never none y-found.

([1] Come round me; [2] all through his life;
[3] kind and polite)

The ballads were poems, partly because poems are easy to remember, partly because they were sung, and partly because the singer or story-teller was often a poet. The singer-poet changed the words from time to time. We must remember that the earliest Robin Hood ballads were sung a long time before there were any printed books in Britain (Caxton printed his first book in 1477).

Some of the stories in this book come from the ballads in *A Little Geste of Robin Hood*, which was printed in 1489 (they are all in the *Oxford Book of Ballads*). Because they come

from very early ballads, you will not find anything in them about Maid Marian, Robin Hood's
clever wife. She came into later ballads, with
the fat and jolly Friar Tuck. Some of the stories
in this book come from these later ballads.

Robin Hood's chief enemy in these stories is
the Sheriff of Nottingham. Robin is also against
some churchmen who grew fat on lands and
money that they took from the people. But he
was not against the church. And we are told
that he loved "Our dear Lady" (the Virgin Mary)
so much that he would not hurt any company in
which there was a woman.

Robin Hood and Little John

Robin Hood was the best bowman in England, and he could fight very well with a sword. There was one other weapon that he could use better than most other men. That weapon was the quarterstaff. It was a yeoman's weapon, but Robin didn't always carry one.

One day, Robin was looking for deer in the forest. He had his sword at his side, his good bow in his hand, and arrows at his back. He saw some deer on the far side of a little river. There was a bridge over the river, but it was only a metre wide, and a man was standing on it.

He was a very big man, much more than two metres tall, and he had a strong quarterstaff.

Robin came to the end of the bridge, but the tall man didn't move.

"Good morning, friend," Robin Hood said. "I want to get to the other side of the river."

The man said nothing, and he didn't move.

Robin put an arrow to his bow, and he said, "Let me come over the bridge."

"You're very brave!" said the big man. "You with your bow and arrow, when I have only a staff!"

"Can you use your staff?" Robin asked. And he went to some young trees and cut a quarter-staff for himself. He left his bow and arrows on the ground, and went back to the bridge. "We'll fight for the bridge," he said. "The one who falls into the river is the loser."

"Ha, ha! Yes!" the big man laughed. "I love a fight. And I hope you love a bath!"

They started to fight. They were both very quick with their weapons. Each tried to hit the other, but each was very quick to stop the other's staff with his own staff.

For an hour they fought, their staves moving very fast. Then at last Robin found an opening. His staff hit the big man on the head.

Robin Hood started to laugh – too soon! The big man's quarterstaff came down on Robin's staff so hard that it broke. The wood was too green. Robin's foot went over the side of the bridge, and he fell into the water.

The big man looked down. "Are you hurt?" he called. "Do you want help?"

But Robin wasn't hurt. As he climbed up the river bank, he was laughing. "That was a good fight," he said. "You're a strong man. Can I do anything for you?"

"Yes," said the big man. "You can help me to find Robin Hood. I want to be one of his men."

Robin Hood sounded his horn, and twenty men in Lincoln green were soon at the bridge.

Will Scarlet said, "You've been in the water,

Robin Hood fights the big man on the bridge

Robin. Did this man throw you in? Shall we throw him into the river, Robin?"

"Robin!" said the big man. "Are you Robin Hood? Have I hit Robin Hood with my quarterstaff? Will you forgive me? I didn't know."

Robin Hood laughed again, and he told his men about the fight on the bridge. "He wants to be one of us," Robin said. "I like you – er – what is your name?"

"My name is John Little."

"Little?" said Robin, laughing because John was so big. "I think we'll call you Little John."

So Little John went with Robin Hood and his men. They made a fire and dried Robin's clothes, and they cooked some good deer meat.

Next morning, at Robin Hood's greenwood tree, Little John was given clothes of Lincoln green and the biggest bow from the outlaws' store.

"I'll teach you to use the bow," said Robin Hood. "You'll soon be a very good bowman because you're so strong and so tall."

Robin Hood and Sir Richard of the Lee

A knight came riding through the forest trees in the greenwood. He rode like a poor man, on an old horse and in old clothes.

Suddenly he heard: "Welcome, good knight! Welcome to the greenwood!"

The knight looked up. Two yeomen in green clothes stood at his horse's head. They had arrows ready to shoot from their long bows.

"Who are you?" the knight asked.

The bigger man answered: "They call me Little John. And my friend here is Much the miller's son. We are Robin Hood's men."

"I know about Robin Hood," said the knight. "He is a good man. He takes money from those who have a lot, but he gives it to the poor. He never takes anything from women or from good yeomen who work in the fields or in the forest."

"That's right," Little John said. "And now will you come with us? Robin is waiting for his dinner. He told us to find somebody to have dinner with him."

"I wasn't going to have any dinner today," the knight said. "I'll come with you gladly."

Little John and Much brought the knight to Robin Hood.

"Welcome, Sir Knight," said Robin.

"I am Sir Richard of the Lee," said the knight.

"Then, Sir Richard, let us have dinner."

It was a very good dinner. There was fish from the river, deer from the forest – as much as the knight could eat.

"I haven't had a dinner like that for a long time, Robin," he said. "Thank you!"

"Do you want to pay something for it?" Robin Hood asked. "If you do, I can give food like that to other people – poor people."

"I'd like to pay," said the knight, "but I don't have much money – only one piece of gold."

Robin looked at him. "If that is all you have, I won't take it. And if you need more, you can have it. But Little John must see."

Little John looked in the knight's bags. "It's right," he said. "The knight doesn't have more than one piece of gold."

"Do you want to tell us why?" Robin asked.

"Yes, Robin," said Sir Richard. "I had a son. He killed a knight. It was in a fair fight at the tournament field, but the proud Sheriff of Nottingham put my son in prison. To get him out of prison took all my money and more. I had to borrow."

"You borrowed from your friends?" Robin said.

"No. When I was rich, I had friends. When I wanted money, they all left me. I had to borrow from the rich abbot of the Abbey of St Mary. I must pay him back four hundred pieces of gold. If I can't pay him back the money tomorrow, he will take my castle and all my lands."

Robin spoke to Little John. "Go to our hiding-place, Little John, and get four hundred pieces of gold. Sir Richard can borrow it from us."

Little John counted out more than four hundred pieces of gold.

"Can't you count?" asked Much.

"This is the way to count money when a poor knight has to have it."

They took the money to Robin Hood.

"Robin," said Little John, "this man is a knight, but his clothes are very old. You must give him the right clothes for a knight. We have good green cloth ..."

"Yes," said Robin. "Give him three metres."

Little John gave the knight four metres of Lincoln green cloth. Then he said, "And the knight must have a good horse, not the old one he came on."

"Yes," said Robin Hood. "Give him a good horse."

Little John gave him Robin's best horse.

Sir Richard of the Lee thanked Robin for all these things. "When must I pay back the money I am borrowing from you?" he asked.

"In one year from today, if you can," said Robin, "under this greenwood tree. Now go and pay the abbot. – And a knight mustn't ride alone. Little John will go with you and help you."

Sir Richard pays
the Abbot

"We must go to York," said Sir Richard of the Lee to Little John. "I must pay the Abbot of St Mary the four hundred pieces of gold tomorrow, or he can take my castle and all my lands."

The next day, the abbot was at dinner in the great hall of his abbey. The Sheriff of Nottingham and many other lords were with him.

Sir Richard of the Lee and Little John came into the hall. The knight went down on his knee in front of the abbot, and said: "Sir Abbot, I borrowed money from you, and today is the day that I must pay it back."

"Have you brought the money?" asked the abbot, and he didn't look pleased.

Sir Richard said nothing.

"No?" said the abbot, and he looked glad. "Then why have you come?"

"Can I ask for more time to pay?" said the knight. "You say you are the servant of God, and in God's name I ask it."

"No," said the abbot. "Your castle and lands are mine now."

Sir Richard asked the sheriff and the other lords to help him.

"No," they all said. "You have lost your

castle and all your lands. Go away."

The knight stood up. "I will pay you your money. And God will judge you because you wanted to take my castle and my lands."

He spoke to Little John, and John counted the four hundred pieces of gold, one at a time, on to the table in front of the abbot: "One piece for the abbot, the servant of God. Two pieces for the abbot. Three pieces for the abbot. Four..." Up to: "Four hundred pieces for the abbot, the servant of God."

Then the knight and Little John went away.

Sir Richard of the Lee went home in his new green clothes. His wife was waiting for him.

"Have we lost everything?" she asked.

"No," he said. "The castle and my lands are ours. But we must thank Robin Hood for that."

The knight stayed in his castle and on his lands, and he worked hard every day. At last he had four hundred pieces of gold. He said to his wife, "Now I have the money that I borrowed from Robin Hood. But I want to take him a present too."

So Sir Richard made a hundred good bows. And his wife and her ladies made a hundred times twenty good arrows.

One year from the day the knight had seen Robin Hood, he went to see him again. He took the four hundred pieces of gold, and the bows and the arrows, and he went into the greenwood.

Little John counts the four hundred pieces of gold

Little John and the Sheriff of Nottingham

Meanwhile, Little John went to shoot, in a tournament with other men, for a gold and silver arrow. He shot very well. His arrows all hit the mark. The Sheriff of Nottingham gave him the gold and silver arrow.

"This is the best bowman I ever saw," the sheriff thought. "Young man," he said to Little John, "what is your name, and where are you from?"

"Men call me Reynold Greenleaf," said Little John, "and I'm from Holderness."

"Well, Reynold Greenleaf," said the proud sheriff, "will you be my man? I will give you good food and clothes, a good horse, and fifteen pieces of gold a year."

"I'm the servant of a good knight," said Little John, "but if he says yes, I'll work for you."

Sir Richard was working in his castle and on his land, and he didn't need Little John. And Robin Hood laughed when John said: "I'll be the worst servant the proud sheriff ever had."

So Little John became the sheriff's man.

One Wednesday, the sheriff went into Sherwood Forest to shoot deer. He thought that "Reynold

Greenleaf" was with his men, but Little John was in bed.

After a time, Little John went to the kitchen, took some food, and sat down to eat it. The sheriff's cook found him there.

The cook was a strong man, and afraid of nobody.

"You take food from my kitchen!" he shouted. "Take that!" And he hit Little John very hard.

Little John jumped up with his sword, but the cook took a sword too. They fought for an hour.

"You're one of the best swordsmen I ever met," said Little John, breathing hard. "If you were as good with a bow, you could come to the greenwood with me. Robin Hood would be glad to see you."

"Robin Hood?" cried the cook. "Reynold Greenleaf, are you Little John? I've heard of you. Stop fighting, and we'll be friends. I hate the sheriff."

They sat down, and the cook brought out the best food and drink in the sheriff's kitchen. Then they went to the sheriff's strong-room, and broke the great doors. There were gold and silver cups and other things, and money: three hundred and three pieces of gold. They took all these things and went to Robin's greenwood tree.

"Welcome," said Robin to Little John, "and welcome to the good yeoman you've brought with you. What's happening in Nottingham?"

"The sheriff sends you presents. Here they are: his cook, and his best cups and other things, and three hundred and three pieces of gold."

"I'd like to thank the sheriff," said Robin.

"Would you?" said Little John. And he ran into the greenwood and found the sheriff.

"Where have you been, Reynold Greenleaf?" asked the sheriff.

"I've been to look for deer for you. And I've found the greatest one in the forest. Will you come with me and see?"

The sheriff rode his horse, and Little John ran, and they were soon at Robin's greenwood tree.

"Here is the greatest one in the forest," said Little John, and he went down on his knee in front of Robin Hood.

"Welcome, Sheriff," said Robin. "You must eat with us here."

The proud sheriff was very angry, but he sat down, and Robin's men brought the food and drink – in the sheriff's best gold and silver things. When he saw them, the sheriff couldn't eat anything.

"Let me go," said the sheriff. "Let me go, and I'll be the best friend you ever had."

"Will you promise," said Robin, "to be my friend, and not to try to catch or kill me? And will you promise to help my men if you see them?"

"I promise."

Little John took the sheriff to the road, and then went back to the greenwood tree.

13

Robin Hood and
Friar Tuck

One beautiful June day, Robin Hood and his merry men were in the forest. They saw a big deer, but it was more than a hundred and fifty metres away.

Little John shot an arrow at it from his big bow, and the deer fell dead.

"That was a good shot, Little John," said Much the miller's son.

"Yes," said Robin Hood. "If we travelled a hundred miles, we wouldn't find a better bowman."

Will Scarlet laughed. "There's a curtal friar at Fountains Abbey," he said. "His name is Friar Tuck, and he is a better bowman than any of us."

"Is that true?" said Robin. "Then I won't eat and I won't drink before I see Friar Tuck."

Robin Hood put an iron cap on his head. He put his sword at his side. Then, with his bow in his hand, he went to Fountains Dale.

In Fountains Dale, beside the river, he saw the curtal friar. Friar Tuck had an iron cap on his head, and a sword at his side.

Robin Hood called out, "Carry me across the river, Friar Tuck, if you want to stay alive."

The friar took Robin on his back, and carried him across the river. He said nothing to him all the way.

Robin jumped down from the friar's back. Friar Tuck quickly drew his sword. "Now, young man," he said, "carry me back over the river, or you'll be sorry."

Robin Hood took Friar Tuck on his back, and carried him across the river. He said nothing to him all the way.

This time, it was Robin who drew his sword. "Carry me over the river, Friar Tuck, if you want to stay alive."

The friar took Robin on his back again. He said nothing to him before they were half-way across the river. And there, in the deepest part, he threw Robin into the water – and fell on top of him. He was a very heavy man.

After that, there was a great sword fight.

From ten o'clock in the morning to four in the afternoon, they fought with their swords. Robin Hood was a very good swordsman, but Friar Tuck was just as good.

At last Robin said, "Can we stop this for a minute? I must sound my horn."

The fight stopped, and Robin Hood sounded his horn three times. Fifty yeomen, with their bows ready, came running down to the river.

"What men are these?" asked Friar Tuck.

"They are my men," said Robin Hood.

"Well, I don't have a horn, and I don't have

fifty bowmen. But let me put two fingers in my mouth. Then we'll see what happens."

Friar Tuck put two fingers in his mouth and sent out a very loud high sound. Fifty great dogs came running to the friar. Two of them went at once to Robin Hood. They took his coat of Lincoln green in their teeth, and tore it off him.

The outlaws couldn't shoot the dogs that were round Robin Hood. The friar had taught all his dogs to catch arrows in their mouths.. Only Little John's arrows flew too fast for them.

"Call your dogs away," shouted Little John. "Call them away, or I'll kill them – and you!" And he began to shoot. Ten of the friar's great dogs were soon wounded or dead.

"Stop, good yeoman," said Friar Tuck. "Whose man are you?"

"I am Little John, Robin Hood's man. You must stop fighting and be his friend."

Friar Tuck had kept Fountains Dale for seven years. No knight or lord had fought with him, and won.

"I'll stop," he said, and he called his great dogs away. "But what do you want?"

Robin Hood answered, "I want you to come with us to Sherwood Forest. You can live with us, and be our outlaw friar. You'll get one gold piece every month, and new clothes three times a year."

And that is how the outlaws got their own friar.

Friar Tuck carries Robin across the river again

How the Abbot's Money came back to Robin Hood

One year from the day Sir Richard of the Lee borrowed four hundred pieces of gold, Robin Hood was waiting for him. He sent his three best bowmen to meet the knight – Little John, and Much the miller's son, and Will Scarlet.

They didn't meet Sir Richard, but they met a fat churchman, a monk.

"Ah!" said Little John. "Do you think this monk is bringing the borrowed money? Have your long bows ready."

There were fifty-two fighting men with the monk, and seven strong horses carried his things. Two boys led the horses.

Little John, Much, and Will Scarlet held their great bows with arrows ready.

"Stop!" cried Little John.

"Who are you?" the monk asked.

"We are Robin Hood's men."

When the fifty-two fighting men heard the name, they ran. Only the two boys stayed with the monk.

Robin's men took the monk and his horses to Robin Hood.

"Welcome, friend," said Robin Hood. "Where are you from?"

"From the Abbey of St Mary."

"Do you have four hundred pieces of gold that my friend Sir Richard of the Lee paid to your abbot?" asked Robin.

"No," said the monk. "I have only fifteen pieces of gold – not a penny more."

"If that is all you have," said Robin, "I won't take a penny. And if you need more, you can have it. But Little John must see."

Little John looked in the monk's bags. "It's right," he said. "He has only fifteen pieces of gold – added to the money the abbot has sent us. The abbot is very kind. He has sent the four hundred pieces of gold the knight borrowed from us, *and* four hundred more! I have counted eight hundred and fifteen pieces of gold."

"Thank your abbot," said Robin Hood. "We will keep the eight hundred pieces of gold, and poor people will be very glad to have it. Take your fifteen pieces. I won't take a penny of that."

The monk rode away, very angry.

Before night fell, Sir Richard of the Lee came to the greenwood tree.

"I am here, Robin Hood," he said. "I have brought the four hundred pieces of gold that I borrowed from you."

Robin Hood said, "The Abbot of St Mary has paid it for you. I won't take it from you as well as from him. That wouldn't be fair. Take back your money, and help poor people with it." He told Sir

19

Richard about the monk, and the knight laughed.

"I know a lot of poor people – sick yeomen and women and children – who need money," he said.

"Help them," said Robin, "and if you want more money for them, tell me. We can always get more from rich lords and rich churchmen. – But, tell me, what are those bows and all those arrows for?"

"They are a present for you and your merry men. My wife and her ladies made the arrows, so they will be good."

"Thank you," said Robin. "And if ever you need help, sound your horn three times, like this." Robin Hood sounded his own horn three times, and a hundred men in Lincoln green came running through the forest.

Robin Hood and
Maid Marian

Some say that Robin Hood was the son of the Earl of Huntingdon. As a boy, Robin lived in his father's castle until his father was killed by the Sheriff of Nottingham.

Not very far away from the Earl of Huntingdon's castle, Lord Fitzwater had a castle. Between the two castles there was a forest. The Earl of Huntingdon's son Robin and Lord Fitzwater's daughter Marian often met in the forest. The boy and the girl became friends. Marian was a pretty girl, but she was also strong. She could use a bow nearly as well as Robin, and he had taught her to use a quarterstaff.

It was a very sad day for Maid Marian when the Sheriff of Nottingham took the Earl of Huntingdon's castle and made young Robin leave it.

For a few years, she heard nothing about Robin. Then, one day, she heard two men talking about the outlaws of Sherwood Forest.

"There are more than a hundred of them," one man said. "They shoot the king's deer, and they take money from the rich."

"Yes," said his friend, "but they give that money to the poor. And they never take anything from women or from poor people or good yeomen. They have a fine leader. His name is Robin Hood, and he is the friend of all good country people."

"They say," the first man added, "that there is no better bowman in the country."

Maid Marian thought about their words. "It sounds like my Robin. I'll go and see this Robin Hood."

She put a boy's clothes on, with a green hood that hid her hair and most of her face. Then, with her bow and arrows and a strong quarterstaff, she left Lord Fitzwater's castle. Nobody saw her go.

A few days after that, Marian was in Sherwood Forest. She was very hungry, and she was glad to see a nice fat deer. With an arrow on the string of her bow, she began to move very quietly through the trees towards the deer.

"Boy!" said a loud voice. "What are you doing?"

Away went the deer! Marian turned quickly. The man whose loud voice had driven away her food was quite near her. He had a big quarterstaff, but he was not carrying a bow, and he had no sword. She couldn't see his face because he was wearing a big hood. He looked very strong, but Marian was angry with him.

"You saw what I was doing," she said, "and you have driven my deer away."

"These are the king's deer, boy! You mustn't shoot them. Go away!"

"I won't go away," said Marian. "I'm not afraid of you. I'm not afraid of any man who hides his face." She dropped her bow and went towards him with her quarterstaff.

The man laughed, and took his quarterstaff in both hands.

It was a good fight. The man was very strong, and his quarterstaff flew through the air very fast. But it was clear that he didn't want to hurt the "boy". His staff often touched Marian, but never hit her really hard. She could move very quickly.

Marian's staff travelled fast too. The man had to use his staff quickly to stop Marian's. And sometimes she was too quick for him, and he got a good bang on the head.

At last the man said, "Let's stop. I'll say I'm sorry about your deer. I like you. You're very young, but you're going to be a fine fighter. Will you come and be one of Robin Hood's merry men?"

Marian threw back her hood. The man stood quite still. Then he threw back his own hood.

"Robin!" cried Marian.

Robin Hood looked at the lovely face and hair of the woman who, as a young girl, had been his little friend.

Robin Hood and Maid Marian came to Robin's greenwood tree. Will Scarlet was there.

"Where's Friar Tuck?" Robin asked.

Maid Marian throws back her hood

"He's gone into the forest to pray," said Will Scarlet, laughing. "He took his bow and arrows with him."

"Please find him and bring him here," said Robin.

Some men ran to find the friar. They soon came back with him. He was carrying a fat deer on his back.

"These men say you want me," he said to Robin Hood. "They stopped my prayers, and I hope there was a good reason for that."

"Yes," said Robin. "Maid Marian and I want you to marry us. Here. Now."

"Maid——?" said Friar Tuck. "I don't see a lady here.

Maid Marian threw back her hood again, and they all saw a beautiful woman's head above the boy's clothes.

Friar Tuck and Robin Hood's merry men shouted in happy surprise.

And that is how Robin Hood and Maid Marian were married in the greenwood. They lived happily there for many years.

Robin Hood and
the Butcher

One day, Robin Hood saw a man riding through the forest. He was on a big horse, with a big basket on each side.

"Good morning!" said Robin. "I like to see a happy man in the forest. Tell me what your work is, and where you live."

The man answered, "I'm not going to tell you where I live, but I'm a butcher. My baskets are full of meat, and I'm going to Nottingham to sell it."

"I would like to be a butcher," said Robin Hood. "How much do you want for your meat and your horse?"

"If you want my meat and my horse, you must pay me two pieces of gold for them."

Robin Hood gladly paid the butcher the money. Then he rode the butcher's horse to Nottingham. When other butchers began to sell their meat, Robin began to sell his.

Soon the other butchers found that they couldn't sell any meat. Robin was selling more meat for a penny than they could sell for five. So they said to each other: "This is a foolish young man who has sold his father's land. He isn't a real butcher."

The other butchers wanted to know more about Robin Hood, so they went to him and said, "We're all butchers, and we must be friends. Will you have dinner with us?"

At that time, the butchers always had dinner in the hall of the Sheriff of Nottingham, and the other butchers took Robin Hood there.

"Bring lots to drink!" said Robin. "I'll pay for it all, even if it adds up to five pieces of gold or more. Drink, my friends, drink!"

"He's a fool," the other butchers said.

The sheriff thought, "This is the son of a rich farmer. He has sold his land for silver and gold, and he wants to live foolishly. I'll get something from the fool." Then to Robin he said, "Do you have any horned beasts that you will sell to me?"

"Yes, a lot," said Robin. "Two or three hundred. And I have a lot of land – good free land. Would you like to see my land and my beasts? They are mine, just as they were my father's, and his father's before him. But I can sell them if you want to buy them."

The Sheriff of Nottingham took three hundred pieces of gold. He rode with Robin to see the "horned beasts" and the land.

Robin led the way into Sherwood Forest.

"Is this the way?" said the sheriff. "God save us from the man they call Robin Hood!"

A little further along the forest road, Robin Hood saw about a hundred good red deer. They came near, and Robin said, "How do you like my horned beasts? They look good and fat, don't they?"

"I don't like this," said the sheriff. "And I don't like you. I'm going back to Nottingham."

Robin Hood sounded his horn three times. Little John came running through the trees at the head of all Robin Hood's merry men.

"What must we do, Robin Hood?" asked Little John.

"I've brought the Sheriff of Nottingham here to have dinner with us."

"He is welcome," said Little John. "I know he has a lot of gold, so he will gladly pay for his dinner. A lot of poor people will have good dinners that the sheriff's gold will buy."

Little John counted out three hundred pieces of gold from the sheriff's bag. But the sheriff didn't want to stay to have dinner.

So Robin Hood led the sheriff through the greenwood to the road. "Goodbye, kind sheriff," said Robin. And he laughed as the sheriff rode away.

Robin Hood and Alan-a-Dale

Robin Hood and Maid Marian were standing under a tree in the greenwood when a young man came along the forest road. The young man was good to see, in his new red clothes. His face was happy, and he was singing merrily.

Next morning, Robin and Marian saw the same young man. He had thrown away his red clothes, he wasn't singing, and his face was very sad.

Little John and Much the miller's son came out from among the trees and stood in front of the young man.

Little John said, "We don't want to hurt you. Just come and speak to our leader, under that greenwood tree."

The young man came and stood unhappily in front of Robin Hood.

Robin spoke kindly to him. "Do you have any money that you don't need? We know a lot of people that need it."

Very sadly the young man said, "I have only ten pence and a gold ring. The ring was for a beautiful young woman. I was going to marry her today, but they have taken her away from me. They are going to marry her to a rich old knight.

I don't want to live without her. Take my ten pence, and let me die."

"Tell me your name," said Robin Hood.

"My name is Alan-a-Dale."

"And you have no money," said Robin Hood, "so what will you give me to get her back for you? I am Robin Hood."

"I have no money, Robin Hood, but I will promise to be your very good servant. I'll be your man for as long as you need me."

"How far away is your lady-love's home, and where is the marriage to be?"

"Her home is an hour's walking from here. The marriage is to be at the church near her home in an hour."

Robin Hood ran with Alan-a-Dale and some of his men. They didn't stop, and they got to the church before anybody. Alan-a-Dale and the outlaws hid, and only Robin went into the church. He took a harp with him, and he waited.

A fat churchman came into the church.

"What are you doing here?" he asked Robin.

"I'm a harper," said Robin. "I'm the best harper in the north of England."

"Oh, welcome!" said the churchman. "I love harp music. What will you play for me?"

Just then, a rich knight came into the church. He was old, and ugly, and fat. A very pretty young woman came and stood unhappily beside him.

"This isn't right!" cried Robin Hood. "This

young woman mustn't marry that old man. It isn't fair. – But I came to make music. Listen."

But they didn't hear Robin's harp. They heard him sound his horn, three times.

Twenty-four brave bowmen came running to the church. And Alan-a-Dale brought Robin's bow and gave it to him. The bowmen stood round the people in church, with arrows ready.

The pretty young woman ran to Alan-a-Dale, and he held her in his arms.

"Marry them," Robin said to the churchman.

"It's not right," the churchman said. "By the laws of the church and by the laws of England, the people in church must be asked three times. Only then can a man and woman be married."

Robin Hood pulled off the churchman's coat, and he put it on Little John. "Now you are a churchman, Little John. Do what must be done."

Little John stood in front of the people in the church. He was a very big man, and the people began to laugh. He asked them seven times. ("Three times doesn't seem very much," he said.)

And then, "Who gives this woman to Alan-a-Dale?" Little John asked.

"I do," said Robin Hood. "And if anybody takes her away from Alan-a-Dale, he'll have to answer to me."

So Alan-a-Dale was married to his lady-love. She looked beautiful in her happiness. And they all went back to the greenwood, to live free in the forest air.

Robin's men come into the church

Robin Hood and the Fat Monks

Robin Hood put on the clothes of a friar and went to the forest road.

A friar should be poor. He should get his food by asking kind people for it. So Robin looked poor in his friar's clothes.

Two big, fat, strong monks came along the forest road on good strong horses. They looked pleased to be alive.

"Good morning," Robin Hood said to them. "Can you give me a penny to buy some bread? Nobody has given me anything today – not a bit of bread or a cup of water. Please give me something."

"Ah!" the fat monks said. "We're sorry for you, but we don't have even a penny. If we had a penny, we would give it to you."

Brave Robin Hood laughed. "I'm afraid that isn't true," he said. "I'll try to show you that it isn't true."

The fat monks kicked their horses, and began to ride away as fast as they could. But Robin could run very fast. He soon caught them. And he pulled them both off their horses.

"Don't hurt us! Don't hurt us!" the fat monks cried.

"No! No! I won't hurt you," said Robin Hood. "I won't hurt you. You don't have any money, and so I am sorry for you. Listen. This is what we must do. We want money – all three of us. So we'll go down on our knees on the grass here – all three of us – and we'll pray. We'll ask Heaven to send us some money. Pray!"

The fat monks couldn't say no. They quickly went down on their knees. "Send us, oh send us," they prayed, "some money for our need!"

They prayed very unhappily. Sometimes they cried.

Robin Hood prayed too, but he didn't pray unhappily. Very happily he sang: "Send us, oh send us some money for our need!"

The three of them prayed like that on the grass for an hour.

"Now," said Robin, "let's see how much money Heaven has sent us for our need. We must be fair about this. If one of us has more than the others, he mustn't keep it for himself."

The two monks put their hands in their pockets. "Oh, nothing! Oh, how sad! Nothing!"

"Nothing?" said Robin Hood. "Nothing, after all that praying? But Heaven is good. I must help you to look." And he looked carefully. There were gold pieces hidden in their clothes. Robin counted five hundred gold pieces on to the grass.

"Oh, well prayed!" he said. "You have prayed so well that each of you must have some of this gold." He gave them fifty pieces of gold each. He kept four hundred pieces of gold for the poor.

The fat monks didn't dare to say anything. They got up from their knees. They wanted to go, but Robin said:

"Wait! This is Heaven's own place, where Heaven sent us gold. You must make promises in a place like this. Promise that you will never say anything untrue again."

They promised.

"Promise that you will not keep your money when poor people need it."

They promised.

Then Robin Hood helped them to get on their horses and go. Robin went back to the greenwood, and he laughed all the way.

Robin Hood in Nottingham

The Sheriff of Nottingham hated Robin Hood. "How can I catch him?" he thought. "I must think. – Ah! He is the best bowman in the land. I'll send out word that there will be shooting on a day in June, with fair play for the bowmen. The best bowman will get a gold arrow from me. Robin Hood will come and shoot because I have promised that there will be fair play. And then I'll take him!"

He got fighting men from all his friends: two hundred horsemen, three hundred bowmen, and a hundred others.

Robin Hood heard about the shooting.

"Get ready," he said to his men. "We'll go to Nottingham, and four of us will shoot."

One hundred and forty strong young men went with Robin. The Sheriff of Nottingham saw only three of Robin's men: Little John, Much the miller's son, and Will Scarlet. They shot well, better than any of the bowmen from other places. But the best was Robin Hood. Every arrow from his bow hit the mark. The gold arrow was his, and he took it from the sheriff with many thanks.

Robin Hood shoots at the mark

The sheriff held up his hand to his swords-men, and they ran to take Robin. But then they stopped. More than a hundred bowmen, with arrows ready, stood out from among the people.

"Don't you remember your promise?" Robin said to the sheriff. "Under my greenwood tree you promised to be my friend."

Some of the sheriff's men began to run away, but some of them stayed. A fight began.

An arrow hit Little John's knee and wounded him badly.

"Please, Robin," he said, "don't let the sheriff take me alive. Kill me with your sword, and leave me dead."

"Never!" said Robin. And he took the big man on his back. All the way from Nottingham to the Lee he carried Little John.

Sometimes he had to put him on the ground to shoot at the men who came after them. Then he took him up again and went on.

They came to a strong castle just inside the forest. It was Sir Richard's castle, and the knight welcomed Robin Hood and all his men.

"I'm not afraid of the Sheriff of Notting-ham," he said. "Come in, and we'll shut up the castle and shoot from the walls."

Robin Hood saves
Sir Richard of the Lee

The Sheriff of Nottingham got more men from his friends. He led them to the castle of Sir Richard of the Lee.

"You are helping the king's enemies," he shouted to Sir Richard. "You must let me come into your castle to take them."

"I don't know that my friends are the king's enemies," Sir Richard answered. "You can't come into my castle. We must know what the king says."

The sheriff rode hard to London. He told the king about Sir Richard, about Robin Hood, and about the brave bowmen. "This Robin Hood is an outlaw," he said. "He and his men shoot your deer in the forest. They take money from lords and good churchmen. They are your enemies, and we must stop them."

"In two weeks," said the king, "I will be in Nottingham. I will take Robin Hood myself, and I will take Sir Richard of the Lee. Ride back now to Nottingham and get bowmen from all the country round."

Meanwhile, the sheriff's men left their places round the castle and went back to Nottingham.

So Robin Hood and his men went into the greenwood.

The Sheriff of Nottingham wanted to catch Robin, but he couldn't. "I can't catch Robin Hood," he thought, "but I can catch Sir Richard of the Lee if he comes out of his castle."

The sheriff sent a man to the knight's castle.

"I come from Robin Hood," said this man. "He needs you. Please come to help him. I'll lead you."

And that is how the Sheriff of Nottingham caught Sir Richard of the Lee. With a lot of soldiers he took the knight along the road to Nottingham. A woman saw them go, and she ran into the greenwood and found Robin Hood.

"Robin Hood," she cried, "they have taken Sir Richard of the Lee!"

"Who has taken him?" asked Robin.

"The Sheriff of Nottingham."

Robin Hood sounded his horn, and more than a hundred men in Lincoln green came running through the trees.

"Will you come with me to Nottingham to save Sir Richard of the Lee?"

They ran through the greenwood and over the fields, their bows in their hands, their arrows on their backs, and their swords at their sides. They ran into Nottingham, and there, in front of them, they saw the Sheriff of Nottingham. All his soldiers were with him, and Sir Richard of the Lee.

"Stop, proud Sheriff!" shouted Robin. "Stop and speak to me. Tell me what the king said to you in London."

"I don't speak to outlaws," said the sheriff. And to the soldiers he said, "Take that man!"

But the soldiers saw a hundred arrows in a hundred bows all round them, and not a man moved.

"I have never run so far or so fast," said Robin Hood. "And I tell you, Sheriff, it is not to do you good."

An arrow flew from Robin's bow, and the sheriff fell dead.

"You must come with us to the greenwood, Sir Knight, and you must stay with us for a time. When the king gives us his pardon, you will have your castle and your lands again."

The King and
Robin Hood

The king came to Nottingham with a great number of knights. He came to take Robin Hood and Sir Richard of the Lee.

"If any man brings me Sir Richard's head," the king said, "I promise to give him Sir Richard's castle and all his lands."

There was a good old knight who heard that, and he said: "My Lord the King, do not give Sir Richard's lands to any man, if you like that man. Nobody in this country can have the knight's lands if Robin Hood is alive and can carry a bow."

"Then we must kill Robin Hood first, mustn't we?" said the king.

The king stayed in Nottingham for many weeks, but nobody could find Robin Hood. Nobody knew where he was. Or if they did know, they didn't say.

At last one of the king's foresters said, "My Lord the King, if you want to see Robin Hood, this is what you must do. Take five of your best knights, and go down to the abbey near the river. Get monks' clothes there, and then take the road to Nottingham. I'll lead you. Before you get to

Nottingham, you will meet Robin Hood if he is alive."

The king put on the clothes of a rich abbot, with a big hat over his hood. His five knights dressed as churchmen too. Then, with horses carrying great bags, they started through the forest. They hadn't gone far in the greenwood when they met Robin Hood – and a few good bowmen with him.

Robin took the king's horse. "Sir Abbot," he said, "please stay for a time. We are yeomen of this forest. We live by shooting the king's deer, and we have no other way of living. But you have churches, and money from the people, and gold. Please give us some of your riches to give to poor people."

The king answered him: "I have only forty pieces of gold. I have been with the king in Nottingham, and that took a lot of my money. If I had a hundred pieces of gold, I would gladly give you fifty for the poor."

Robin took the forty pieces of gold and gave half to Little John. Then he gave half back. "Take this, Sir Abbot," he said. "You will need it. We'll meet again."

"Thank you," said the king. "But I bring a word from our lord the king. Look, this is his ring. He asks you to come to Nottingham to have dinner with him."

When Robin saw the king's ring, he went down on his knee. "I love no man in the world," he said, "so well as I love my king. Thank you, Sir Abbot, for your words, and today you must have dinner with me under my greenwood tree." And he led the king there.

The king saw men working to make food ready.

"Are these all your men?" he asked.

Robin sounded his horn three times, and a hundred young men in Lincoln green came running, and stood in lines in front of Robin.

"I like this," the king thought. "He rules his men better than I can rule mine."

The dinner was soon ready – good deer meat, fine bread, and good drink. The king ate and drank well.

"Now, Sir Abbot," said Robin, "you must see how we play."

He and his men jumped up, with their bows in their hands. ("Are they going to shoot me?" the king asked himself.) Then very quickly they put up two marks for shooting. ("The marks are small, and fifty metres away," the king thought. "Can they hit them as far away as that?") Then, two at a time, they shot arrows at the marks. If a man's arrow didn't hit the mark, he had to go on one knee and take his hood off. Then the other man hit him as hard as he could on the head.

The last man to shoot was Robin himself. Four times his arrow went straight to the mark. But the light wasn't so good now, and his last arrow didn't hit the mark.

Robin went on one knee in front of the king and pulled his hood off. "Sir Abbot," he said, "I haven't hit the mark, so somebody must hit me. Will you do it?"

"I don't want to hurt a good yeoman," said the king.

"Don't be afraid to hurt me," said Robin.

The good king took off his coat and hood to free his arm. Then he hit Robin so hard that he fell to the ground.

"You are strong, Sir Abbot," Robin laughed. "Can you shoot well too?"

But then he saw Sir Richard of the Lee. Sir Richard was on his knee in front of the king. He had seen the king's face.

Robin saw too. "My Lord the King of England, now I know you!"

All the outlaws went on their knees.

Robin Hood said, "I ask your pardon, my Lord the King, for me and my men. We are your true servants. Will you pardon us?"

"Yes," said the king. "I have been learning about you. That is why I came here. And now I know about you. I pardon you if you will leave the greenwood – you and all your men – and come and live with me in London. I need men like you around me."

"I'll come to London with you, and I'll bring a hundred men. But if I'm not happy there, I'll have to come back to the greenwood – and shoot more of your deer."

The king eats with Robin and his men

Robin Hood goes
to London

"Do you have any green cloth to sell me?" asked the king.

He and all his knights were soon dressed in Lincoln green. Then the king and his knights, with Robin Hood and his merry men, went to Nottingham.

The people of Nottingham saw a great number of men in green. "Our king is dead," they thought, "and Robin Hood has come to town. He has had enemies here, and he has come to punish us." They began to run away.

The king laughed. "Come back, good people of Nottingham," he shouted. "Are you afraid of your king?"

The people were glad when they saw the king. They brought food and drink. Then they all – king, knights, townspeople and outlaws – ate and drank and sang happily.

Before the king went to London, he sent for Sir Richard of the Lee.

"You have your castle and your lands again," the king said. "Stay here and help my people."

Robin Hood stayed in London for a year. It was not a happy year for him. The king was kind, and the lords and knights listened to him and liked him. But London town was not the greenwood that Robin loved.

At the end of the year, only two of his men were still with Robin Hood in London: Little John and Will Scarlet. The others had come, one by one, to Robin and said: "I love you Robin, but the town is not for me. I want to go back to the greenwood and the open air and the trees."

And Robin Hood had said to each of them, "I know. Go back and be happy. Help the poor, and the old, and all women. Goodbye."

At last Robin Hood himself went to the king.

"My Lord the King," he said, "I must go to the church in Barnesdale. I go there every year to ask pardon for the wrong I have done."

"It's right to do that," said the king. "Go to Barnesdale, but come back to see me when you can."

When Robin got to the greenwood on a fine sunny morning, he heard the merry singing of the birds. "It's a long time since I was here," he thought. "I must shoot a deer to remember old times."

He shot a very big deer, and then he sounded his horn. All the outlaws in the forest knew that sound, and soon a hundred fine young men came through the trees. They went down on their knees to Robin.

"Welcome!" they cried. "Welcome to our dear Robin Hood under the greenwood tree!"

The Death of Robin Hood

Robin Hood and Maid Marian grew old at last. Maid Marian died first, and Robin was alone.

"I can't shoot well," he said to Little John. "My arrows don't fly so straight. I think I'm ill. I'll go to the priory in Kirkleys, the house of women who work for the church. The head of that house, the prioress, is my aunt's daughter, and she will know how to make me well."

"Don't go," said Little John. "Don't go without fifty of your best bowmen."

But Robin said, "I don't want you or anybody to go with me. The prioress and the other women in the priory are the servants of God, and they won't hurt me."

So Robin Hood went alone to Kirkleys, and called at the strong black door.

The prioress came down to see him.

"Yes," she said, "you are ill. You have too much blood in your body, and I must take some of it out."

She took Robin Hood to a little room. She drove a small pointed iron into his arm, and the good red blood began to come out. She stayed with him for an hour – and then for another hour. She didn't stop the blood, and at last Robin knew that she wanted to kill him. She was working for his enemies.

The prioress went out of the room. Robin's blood was still running out. He tried to stop it, but he couldn't. He tried to open the door, but the prioress had locked it. The window was high up, and he was too weak to get to it.

His horn was at his side, and he sounded it three times. The sound was very weak, but Little John heard it. He was under a tree, just outside Kirkleys.

The big man ran to the priory. He broke the strong black door, and he broke other doors inside. At last he broke the door of Robin's room.

Robin was near to death.

"Oh, Robin, Robin," cried Little John. "This is a bad place. I'll carry you out, and then I'll come back – and burn Kirkleys to the ground, and all the bad women in it."

"No, Little John," said Robin, "you mustn't do that for me. I'm dying, but I never hurt a woman in my life. Don't hurt even the prioress. But give me my bow and a good arrow. I'll shoot the arrow through the window, and you can bury me in the ground where the arrow falls. Bury me with green grass under my head, and green grass at my feet. Bury my long bow at my side, and put these words above me:

Here lies brave Robin Hood.

Robin asks Little John for his bow

Questions

Questions on each story

Robin Hood and Little John
1 Why did Robin Hood want to go across the bridge? (Because . . .)
2 Where did Robin Hood and the big man fight?
3 Who fell into the water?
4 What happened when Robin sounded this horn?

Robin Hood and Sir Richard of the Lee
1 What was the big yeoman's name?
2 Where did the yeomen take the knight?
3 What did the Sheriff of Nottingham do to the knight's son?
4 How much money did the knight borrow from the abbot?

Sir Richard pays the Abbot
1 Where was the abbot?
2 What did Sir Richard ask the abbot for?
3 Who counted out the money?
4 Who made the arrows?

Little John and the Sheriff of Nottingham
1 Who won the gold and silver arrow?
2 Who had a sword fight in the sheriff's kitchen?
3 How much money did they take to the greenwood?
4 What did the sheriff promise?

Robin Hood and Friar Tuck
1 Where was Friar Tuck?
2 What did Friar Tuck do half-way across the river?
3 Why did the dogs come to Friar Tuck? (Because . . .)
4 What had Friar Tuck taught his dogs to do?

How the Abbot's Money came back to Robin Hood
1 Who were Robin Hood's three best bowmen?
2 Which abbey was the monk from?

3 How much money did he have?
4 How much did Robin keep for the poor?

Robin Hood and Maid Marian
1 Why did Robin leave his father's castle? (Because . . .)
2 What clothes did Marian wear when she went to the forest?
3 Why didn't she know Robin Hood at first?
4 Why did Robin send for Friar Tuck? (Because . . .)

Robin Hood and the Butcher
1 How much did Robin Hood pay the butcher?
2 Where did the butchers have dinner?
3 What were Robin's "horned beasts"?
4 How much money did they take from the sheriff?

Robin Hood and Alan-a-Dale
1 Why did Alan-a-Dale have a ring?
2 Who went into the church first?
3 Who was the pretty young woman?
4 Who were married in the church?

Robin Hood and the Fat Monks
1 How should a friar get his food?
2 What did Robin and the monks pray for?
3 How much money did the monks take away?
4 What promises did the monks make?

Robin Hood in Nottingham
1 Who won the gold arrow at Nottingham?
2 Why did the sheriff's men stop?
3 What happened to Little John?
4 Where did Robin carry Little John?

Robin Hood saves Sir Richard of the Lee
1 Why did the sheriff ride to London?
2 Why did Robin and his men go into the greenwood?
  (Because. . .)
3 Who told Robin about Sir Richard?
4 What happened to the sheriff?

The King and Robin Hood
1 What clothes did the king put on at the abbey?
2 What did he show to Robin Hood?

3 What happened when Robin Hood sounded his horn?
4 Why did Sir Richard go down on his knee?

Robin Hood goes to London
1 Why did the people think the king was dead? (Because . . .)
2 What did the king tell Sir Richard to do?
3 How many of Robin's men stayed in London for a year?
4 What did Robin do to remember old times?

The Death of Robin Hood
1 Where did Robin Hood go when he was ill?
2 Why did Little John hear Robin's horn?
3 What did Little John want to do to the priory?
4 Where did Robin Hood want to be buried?

Questions on the whole book

These are harder questions. Read the Introduction, and think hard about the questions before you answer them. Some of them ask for your opinion, and there is no fixed answer.

1 These stories began as poetry. This means that some words and expressions are used quite often in the stories, for example "the greenwood/under the greenwood tree". Can you find another word or expression which comes in several places because the stories were ballads?

2 Can you find another way that you can tell that the stories were ballads?

3 Name three people you like in these stories, and say why you like them.

4 Name three people you don't like, and say why you can't like them.

5 Don't answer this question: what did Robin Hood do in the winter? Ask three other questions that have come to your mind in reading these stories.

6 Children like the Robin Hood stories. Why do you think they do?

7 Which story do you like best in this book? Why?

New words

abbey
an important place where an **abbot** and other servants of God live

abbot
an important servant of God

borrow
take something that you will give back

butcher
a person who kills animals and sells their meat

castle
a place with strong walls that soldiers can hold

deer
a forest animal with long horns

enemy
a person or people who will fight against you

fair
just; the same to everybody

friar
one of a group of servants of God who had to help people; a **curtal friar** wore a short coat to work out-of-doors

harp
a musical instrument with a lot of strings

hate
dislike very strongly, and sometimes want to kill

horn
one of the two hard points on the head of a cow, deer, etc; one of these that you blew to call people; **horned** = with horns

judge
say what the punishment must be

knight
a horse-riding leader of soldiers

lord
a man who rules others

meanwhile
at the same time

merry
happy; laughing often

monk
a servant of God

outlaw
a man who had broken the law

pardon
: forgiveness; not wanting to punish

pence
: pennies; a small amount of money

prison
: a strong building where lawbreakers are locked up

promise
: say that you will certainly do something

proud
: feeling important; showing that you are great

quarterstaff
: a thick straight stick, about two metres long, used for fighting. It is also called a **staff** (plural: **staves**)

tournament
: a meeting to find out who is best at a game or sport

welcome
: say that you are glad someone has come

wound
: hurt with a sword, arrow, etc

yeoman
: a working countryman